# SOUTHPAW

# WINNING SEASON

# SOUTHPAW

## RICH WALLACE

SCHOLASTIC INC.
New York Toronto London Auckland Sydney
Mexico City New Delhi Hong Kong Buenos Aires

ISBN-13: 978-0-439-89567-5
ISBN-10: 0-439-89567-7

12 11 10 9 8 7 6 5 4 3 2 1          7 8 9 10 11 12/0

Printed in the U.S.A.          40

First Scholastic printing, April 2007

Set in Caslon 224 Book

FOR SANDRA

# SOUTHPAW

# · CONTENTS ·

# 1
# Cow-Country Pitcher

**J**immy stepped off the mound and jogged toward the dugout, being careful not to step on the first-base line. That'd be bad luck. He was excited now. He'd done well on this first afternoon of tryouts.

The day was overcast and cool, and a few small patches of snow were still melting in the shady spots near the left-field fence. But the baseball diamond was clear and mostly dry. A trickle of sweat ran from Jimmy's unruly hair onto his cheek. He quickly wiped it away.

The muscular kid that Jimmy had just struck

out was frowning as he put his bat in the rack. "What was your name again?" the kid asked.

Jimmy tossed his mitt onto the rickety wooden bench and smiled. Not many kids had bothered talking to him since his arrival in town. "Jimmy Fleming," he said eagerly. "My friends back home call me Flem."

The kid made a sour face and said, "Flem?" He thought for a second, squinting and giving the lanky newcomer a good looking-over. "I don't know where 'back home' is, but to me phlegm is something you hack up and spit out." And he did just that to demonstrate.

"Home is Pennsylvania. And yeah, I've heard all the jokes," Jimmy said, looking away. "They never bothered me."

The other kid shrugged. "I'm Spencer Lewis," he said, not smiling. "But you already knew that."

"I did?"

"You ought to."

Jimmy raised his eyebrows. "That so?"

"Starting shortstop. Leadoff hitter."

"Wow," Jimmy said with a lot of sarcasm. This

kid seemed pretty full of himself. Jimmy decided to needle him a bit. "So I struck out a big star, huh?"

Spencer winced but gave a half-smile. "I ain't hearing that noise," he said. "Everybody knows the pitchers are ahead of the hitters in March. It might take me a minute to get used to a southpaw like you, with that weird left-handed delivery, but tomorrow will be different."

The coach had said there'd be a full week of tryouts before he cut the roster to eighteen players. Jimmy had counted twenty-nine out for the squad.

"The team's pretty well set, you know," Spencer said. "Especially my boys on the pitching staff."

"I think I got a shot," Jimmy replied. He could see that Spencer was going to keep busting his chops, letting him know he was an outsider.

"You got okay stuff. We might be able to use you some in relief."

Jimmy gave Spencer a mean look. "I guess the coaches'll decide that, won't they?"

Spencer shrugged. "Yeah. But they want guys who are gonna fit in, Flem. People who know the score."

"I been pitching for four years," Jimmy said.

"Yeah, in the sticks."

"Sticks? Where'd you find a word like that? 1920?"

"What do you call it?"

"Home."

"Call it whatever you want," Spencer said. "All I'm saying is there's a big difference between Hudson City and cow country."

That stung a little. There actually had been a dairy farm about two hundred yards from the Flemings' house in Pennsylvania. Jimmy's mother owned a horse that she boarded there.

Jimmy just smiled, went into a batting stance, and gave a gentle swing. "Strike three," he said.

"Like I was saying, I ain't used to lefties right now."

"And like I said, I think I got a shot. Besides, you ever heard of Christy Mathewson?" he asked, referring to the Hall of Fame pitcher who had grown up in northeastern Pennsylvania.

"Yeah. So?"

"Where do you think he's from?"

Spencer laughed. "That was, like, forever and two days ago, Flem."

Head Coach Wimmer walked over and cleared his throat. He was old and paunchy and had been leading the Hudson City Middle School seventh-grade team for more than thirty years. "All right, boys," he said, eyeing the bunch. "Pretty good for a first day. You're not quite ready for Yankee Stadium, but we'll whip you into shape.

"Go on home, lay off the ice cream, and be back here after school tomorrow." Coach took off his cap and rubbed his big, bald head. His pink ears stuck out like rounded fins. "And tuck in those shirts; probably be some Major League scouts hanging around looking for prospects. Don't want them to think I run a sloppy ship."

Jimmy laughed with the rest of them, then left the dugout and headed for home, just a short block down 15th Street to the Boulevard.

It still seemed strange to be walking these streets, so noisy and busy with traffic. It had only been a month since he and his dad moved here, taking a second-story apartment above the *Lindo Música Internacional* store. So many things had changed so quickly.

His parents' divorce hadn't been such a surprise; he'd figured it was coming. But he never thought his dad would be leaving Sturbridge, Pennsylvania, to take a job in Jersey City. So Jimmy was left with the biggest decision of his life: Stay with his mother or leave with his dad, right in the middle of seventh grade.

And here he was, suddenly a city dweller, stuck in that urban stretch of North Jersey between the Lincoln and Holland Tunnels, an arm's reach across the Hudson River from the New York City skyline. In a town where half the signs were in Spanish and white kids like him were a minority.

He needed to make the school baseball team. When he gripped that ball this afternoon, pushed back his cap and peered in at the catcher, he'd finally felt at home for a few minutes. When he let loose with that wide overhand delivery and sent the ball zipping toward the plate for the first time this season, he'd felt a burden lifting.

But maybe Spencer was right. Jimmy had been on enough sports teams to know that the coaches often did have their rosters picked way in advance, with few real opportunities for a newcomer to fit in. He'd have to do a lot better than the established players to secure a place on the team.

# 2
# Volume Control

Jimmy always got home before his father—
who commuted by bus to Jersey City—so he'd
do his homework and watch TV or read sports
magazines and comic books. Dad would get home
at about six o'clock and make dinner; he was a
good cook and could whip up some chicken and
vegetables in a hurry. Then they'd hang out in the
sparsely furnished apartment till bedtime.

Once a week or so they'd go to the coin laun-
dry down the street to wash their clothes. And on
Thursdays they'd walk a couple of blocks and get
Chinese or Mexican food in cardboard containers
to go.

The apartment was narrow and long, only about eighteen feet wide. There were two front windows looking out over the Boulevard, with the fire escape zigzagging down the front of the building. Jimmy liked to sit in the living room and watch the traffic on the street while his dad watched TV.

"Hey, Jim, watch this," Dad said, pointing the remote control toward the screen. "This Mets pitcher has the same delivery you've got, but he's smoother, see. You watching?"

Jimmy had been watching passengers unloading from a New Jersey Transit bus. He turned toward the TV and nodded. "He's taller, too."

"Well, yeah, he's an adult. But he's built like you, all arms and legs. And he's a lefty, too. But see how he gets himself planted after the pitch, ready in case the ball gets smacked right back to him? You come down off balance. You gotta work on that."

"I know."

Lean and limber like Jimmy, Dad was built like a first baseman or a hurdler, and he tried to be both at one time or another back in high school.

9

But he hadn't had much success at either. It was no secret that he'd wanted to be a star pitcher. Or that now he wanted Jimmy to be.

Between pitches of the Mets game, Dad flipped over to the Yankees. It was still spring training for the pros, but there were games on every night. Mr. Fleming usually watched two games at once. "You can see almost every pitch if you time it right," he'd say.

The only frustration was the volume. He'd discovered that 18 was the right volume for the Mets games, but that was too loud when he switched channels to the Yankees. He'd click it down to 16, but that seemed a little too soft. The perfect volume for the Yankees' channel was 17, but he'd never leave it at an odd number like that. So he lived with it at 18, despite the discomfort of the slightly-too-high volume.

One other thing about the noise level in the apartment: Even with the TV on, you could hear the music coming from the store downstairs. They were used to it, and the store closed at nine. So it never interfered with their sleep.

When both games were between innings and car commercials were playing, Jimmy asked his dad to switch to the weather station. "I'm hoping it'll be a little warmer tomorrow," he said. "I'll be able to get in a better flow at the tryouts."

The local forecast was just beginning as Dad switched. "Perfect timing," he said with a grin, and though it was just music playing over a printed forecast, Dad upped the volume to 21.

"How come twenty-one is okay?" Jimmy asked. "That's an odd number."

"It's divisible by seven," Dad said. "Twenty-one is three touchdowns and three extra points. So it's not a problem."

"And twenty-five is fine, too?"

"It's symmetrical: five times five. But that's almost always too loud anyway." Dad took off his glasses and rubbed his eyes. "I'll explain it again. The acceptable volume range, depending on the station, is fourteen to twenty-five. All even numbers are okay, plus twenty-five."

"And twenty-one."

"Yes. As I just explained."

"So we can't watch TV at fifteen, seventeen, nineteen, or twenty-three?"

"Right. We can watch those channels, but not at those volumes."

"I got it."

Dad switched back to the Yankees. "Now watch how Menendez follows through. He's a righty, but his mechanics are sound. See? Immediately into a defensive stance after the delivery. You gotta work on that, be ready for a line drive or a grounder."

Jimmy nodded but looked back to the street. Two kids a little older than he was were standing outside Tienda de Amigo, a men's clothing store. One was dribbling a basketball and the other was drinking a bottle of soda. A younger kid whizzed past on a skateboard. Above the store, in an apartment that mirrored his own, a woman was preparing dinner.

Dad took a handful of pretzels from the bag that was next to him on the couch and began to chew very slowly and carefully. It was another of his little quirks—always mindful of making too much noise.

"Dad, just chew 'em normal!" Jimmy said. "It ain't gonna bother me."

"You want to hear the game, don't you?"

"Which game? I can't concentrate on two of 'em at once like you can."

"Like I said, if you time it right—"

"You can see every pitch. I know." Jimmy got up and walked toward his bedroom.

"Where you going?" Dad asked.

"I'll be back in a while."

He left the tiny living room and walked through the kitchen, where the faucet was dripping steadily. His small bedroom was beyond the bathroom, with its flickering overhead light. Across the hall was his dad's room, the length of Jimmy's room and the bathroom combined but still only seven feet wide.

That was the whole place. The door between the bedrooms opened to a narrow stairwell, down to the alley behind the building and up to the third-floor apartment of Mrs. Murphy, an old woman who lived alone with the two cats she wasn't supposed to have. The landlord, Mr. Espino, knew about the cats but let it slide because Mrs. Murphy was such a good tenant otherwise.

Jimmy was feeling antsy. There was so much going on out there on the street, but he was trapped in here, in an apartment that wasn't much bigger than the garage at their house back in Pennsylvania. Except for school and now baseball tryouts, he wasn't allowed to go out on his own. "Not until we know the town a little better," Dad had said. "When you get a little older."

*I'll be fifty before I figure this town out*, he thought. But there was something about the place he liked—the energy especially, the faster pace. Kids around here were streetwise. He wouldn't mind learning some of the ropes himself.

As Spencer had said, Jimmy Fleming needed to know the score.

# 3
# Bringing Up Flem

*I*t was the worst kind of day for baseball—
temperature in the mid-thirties, a misty rain
making everything slippery and cold. Jimmy
rubbed his hands together quickly, trying to gen-
erate some warmth as he waited in the on-deck
circle for Willie Shaw to finish his at-bat.

The week had flown by, and he'd shown what
he could do, fielding most of what was hit to him,
handling most of the batters he faced when called
on to pitch, and getting in some decent cuts at the
ball when he took his turns at bat.

By his estimation, he was better than at least

half the players trying out, and as good as most of the others. Even so, he had no idea if he was going to make the team. He wanted to leave an impression with these last swings of the week.

Willie hit a soft fly ball that barely left the infield. Second baseman Lamont Wilkins trotted slowly backwards and got under it, making the catch.

Jimmy stepped up to the plate and took a practice swing. Out on the mound was Ramiro Velez, who took the throw from Lamont and kicked at the dirt with his toe.

Velez peered in and smirked at Jimmy. They had some classes together and had spoken briefly a couple of times this week. Nothing more than a "How's it going?" or "Crappy weather again."

Jimmy could hit from either side of the plate, but Ramiro was a right-hander, so he decided to bat lefty.

At shortstop, Spencer suddenly made an exaggerated hacking in his throat, pretending to bring up spit. "Heavy phlegm alert," he said loudly.

The catcher, Jared Owen, made the same

noise. Immediately all of the infielders followed suit. More or less in unison, they chanted, "Let's go, Flem!" then made a loud spitting sound and laughed.

Jimmy turned toward Coach Wimmer, who was standing in the dugout. He was shaking his head but grinning. He caught Jimmy's eye and said, "Looks like you're developing a fan club."

Ramiro was laughing too hard to pitch.

"Let's see some action!" Coach yelled.

Ramiro bit down on his lip and nodded. The infielders switched to a more standard baseball chatter: "No batter, no batter, hey batter!"

Jimmy exhaled hard and went into his batting stance, tensed but alert, ready for the pitch.

Ramiro looked in at the catcher, went into his windup, and unleashed a fastball, a little low and inside, but hittable.

Jimmy swung and made contact, but the ball skipped out of bounds before reaching first base. He set the bat between his knees, rubbed his stinging hands again, and adjusted his batting helmet.

The second pitch was a curve, low and outside,

and Jimmy gave it a good look but didn't swing.

The rain was coming down harder now and he could hear it pinging against his helmet.

The "No batter, no batter" chant started up again, but that didn't bother him. Every batter got razzed like that in baseball. The phlegm business was different, and he couldn't quite tell if it was good-natured or slightly vicious. Maybe a little of both.

The third pitch was a fastball right down the middle, and he timed his swing well. The bat met the ball and sent it sailing down the right-field line, high and deep. It was out of the park for sure, but at the last second it drifted foul. Jimmy was nearly to first base, but he had his eyes on the ball.

He trotted back to the plate and picked up his bat, wiping some mud off the grip and onto his sweatshirt.

"Nice cut," said the catcher.

"Thanks."

*Just straighten it out*, Jimmy thought. *Another one like that.*

And here came the pitch, another fastball, a

little lower. Jimmy took a hefty swing and was shocked to meet nothing but air. The ball smacked into Jared's glove. Strike three.

He shut his eyes for a second and blew out his breath. Then he turned and walked back to the dugout.

"That's it for today!" called Coach Wimmer. "We'd need webbed feet if we stay out here any longer."

The players ran in from the field and took shelter in the dugout. Jimmy found a seat and leaned back against the wall.

Ramiro came in smiling and squeezed between David Choi and Jimmy. "Mowed you down, Flem," he said with a smile.

"I think that wind helped you out," Jimmy replied. "That drive to right should have been gone."

Ramiro laughed, revealing his slightly crooked teeth. "The wind's blowing the other way, *muchacho*. It would have been *more* foul if it wasn't."

Coach held up his hand to stop all the chatter. "Nice workout, boys," he said. "Now listen, I'll be posting the roster outside my classroom on Mundy morning, so be sure to check it. If you're not listed, don't be discouraged; just work on your skills, get yourself into a summer league later this year, and try out for the eighth-grade team next spring. The rest of you, I'll see you at practice."

Jimmy felt his stomach sink when Coach mentioned the roster. He glanced around at the other players. There were three or four who were certain to get cut and ten or twelve who wouldn't, but after that it seemed to be a toss-up. And Spencer had been right; there were a number of good pitchers.

Jimmy pulled up the hood of his sweatshirt and followed Ramiro out of the dugout. Ramiro was shorter and had thick black hair. He turned and held up his hand for a high five. "Just busting you about that foul ball," he said. "I thought it was gone."

"Me, too."

"Just straighten it out."

"Easy for you to say."

Coach was stuffing some baseballs into a duffel

bag near home plate. He looked up at Jimmy and Ramiro as they walked by. "We're bound to get some baseball weather soon, huh?"

"You said it," Ramiro replied. "Spring starts next week, don't it?"

"Yep. Mundy. See you guys then."

"You mean at practice?" Jimmy asked.

"What else would I mean?"

"You mean I made it?"

Coach looked around, then nodded quickly and said, "Yep. I see you two as my top relief pitchers. A righty and a lefty."

Jimmy pumped his fist and then slapped hands with Ramiro, who was beaming.

"Keep it quiet, though," Coach said. "Don't go blabbing about that this weekend." He rolled his eyes. "Me and my big mouth . . . That's confidential. Everybody else has to wait."

"We won't say a word," Ramiro said. "But man, this is hype. I got cut last year *and* the year before. I was sure it'd happen again."

"You must have worked in the off-season," Coach said.

"Every day. . . . Most days, anyway."

"It paid off. Now get out of here before we all drown."

Jimmy and Ramiro hustled off the field together. "Which way you headed?" Ramiro asked.

"Down to the Boulevard and a block over."

"I can go that way. Come on."

They ran to the Boulevard and waited for the light to change, then dashed across and headed for the back of Jimmy's building. "You wanna get out of the rain for a few minutes?" Jimmy asked.

Ramiro shrugged. "I'll just get soaked again. I got like six more blocks to go. . . . Maybe get a drink, though, if that's okay."

"Sure."

Jimmy was surprised to hear something frying in the kitchen and the TV on.

"Dad?"

"Came home early," Dad said, poking his head into the hallway. "Wanted to hear how it went."

"It went good. This is Ramiro."

"Howdy, Ramiro. You guys make the team?"

"Looks like it," Jimmy said.

Dad's whole face brightened, and he raised both fists. "No kidding? You a starting pitcher?"

"Reliever."

"Awesome." Dad gave his son a hug and turned to Ramiro. "You made it, too?"

"Yeah."

Jimmy broke loose and grabbed some paper towels, wiping his head and handing some to Ramiro.

"Thanks," Ramiro said.

"What position are you, Ramiro?" Dad asked.

"Same as this guy. We'll both be in the bullpen, it looks like."

"I'll tell you what: You show your stuff in relief, then they'll have to make you starters."

"They already got good starters, Dad," Jimmy said. He was glad enough to have made the team. No reason for his dad to go overboard about it.

"You'll show 'em," Dad said. "Be sure to call your mother and let her know you made it."

Ramiro gave Jimmy a questioning look.

Jimmy felt his stomach squirm a little. "She's in Pennsylvania."

"Oh."

"You still thirsty?"

"Maybe just some water, quick. *My* mother's in Hudson City, and she'll be wondering where I am."

"What are you doing tomorrow?" Jimmy asked.

"Working."

"Working?"

"Yeah. I wash dishes and stuff at my uncle's restaurant, Jalapeños." Ramiro drank the water quickly and glanced at the clock above the stove. "I gotta go," he said. "See you Monday."

"Wait."

"What?"

"You mean *Mundy.*"

They both laughed. "Yeah," Ramiro said. "Sundy, Mundy, Tuesdy."

Jimmy went to the front window and watched Ramiro run up the Boulevard.

"Guess we could have given him a ride," Dad said.

"Yeah."

"I wasn't thinking. Was too excited that you

made the team. Now things will really happen for you. Mark my words: If you keep working, you'll be a star."

Jimmy nodded. He didn't care that much about being a star. He just loved to play. More importantly, he was glad to be on a team again.

"Yep," Dad said. "Just keep working. Saddle up and go, right?"

"Right, Dad."

Dad was always saying things like that, catchphrases that made sense in a weird way. "Saddle up and go" meant something like "Face up to a challenge" or "Get on with it." Dad said those things, too, but "Saddle up and go" seemed to speak for them all.

Jimmy headed for the bathroom to take a shower. He was cold and wet and muddy, but Dad was right. Things were definitely starting to happen.

# 4

# *Arroz con Pollo*

J immy had trouble falling asleep that night, but he decided not to fight it. The rain was steady and it was blowing hard against his bedroom window, which looked across the alley to an apartment house.

He'd called his mom and that had been okay, but those conversations always left him feeling uneasy. She was only a hundred miles away, but she might as well have been on the moon. His only access to her was the telephone or e-mail. Besides, she had always seemed more interested in riding her horse than being with him or his dad. She almost never came to his athletic events when he lived there. His dad always did.

But he had heard something in her voice tonight, a sadness over the fact that he wasn't with her. He'd tried all month to be upbeat about the new situation, but today's news about making the team was the first really good thing that had happened to him in Hudson City.

He still felt bad sometimes for choosing his dad over his mom, choosing a very different environment over the cozy little town in Pennsylvania where he'd lived his entire life. But home was with his father, wherever that might be. He'd even heard his mother say it several times: "The boy needs his dad."

It was true. As eccentric as Dad was—with all his symmetrical rules and quirky expressions—he certainly cared about his son. Sometimes it almost seemed like he cared too much, as if he thought Jimmy would shatter if his dad wasn't there to guide him through the world.

Dad had grown up in New Jersey and had moved "out to the country" before Jimmy was born. When he lost his job in the bookkeeping department of a Scranton manufacturer—"down-sized" they called it, but they all knew a firing when they saw one—he'd taken an offer from a high-school friend and gone to work in Jersey City.

"This will be home," he'd said to Jimmy. "You'll see."

But it wasn't home, and they both knew it. Jimmy hadn't had a lot of friends in Pennsylvania, but he did have some. Here, Ramiro was the first kid to show any interest at all, and that was part-ly from the excitement of making the team.

A truck was idling in the street below Jimmy's window, and a couple of dogs were barking back and forth nearby. Headlights from the Boulevard lit up his walls every few seconds.

He pictured himself out on the mound, the sun blazing, spectators cheering, a bright red HUDSON CITY logo across his uniform chest. The bases were loaded with nobody out, and he'd been summoned from the bullpen to save the game. He threw a strike. Then another and another. One out. The fans were standing now, too excited to sit.

Two quick strikes on the next batter, then a surprise throw to the first baseman, catching the runner off guard and picking him off. Two down.

One more pitch would finish this thing. He wiped his brow, shook off a sign from the catcher, then nodded. He leaned back, went into his windup, and hurled one so fast that the batter never saw it coming. Strike three. Game over. His teammates rushed to the mound and embraced him.

A smile crossed his face and he shut his eyes and relaxed. But someone gunned the engine of the truck downstairs and it backed up noisily, jolting him from the imaginary ballgame.

Jimmy looked over at the clock on his bedside table: 11:52. Tomorrow was Saturday so it didn't matter if he slept in, but his dad had to work. What would he do by himself? No way was he sitting inside all day.

He pulled a blanket over his head and tried to drift off to sleep. Sooner or later, he did.

\* \* \*

The sun was shining when he woke the next morning, and he could hear music from a car radio in the alley. His stomach was rumbling with hunger.

"Nine forty?" he said aloud as he looked at the clock. "That's about the latest I ever slept."

Dad had left a note that he'd be home by four, and also a twenty-dollar bill. *Get milk and oranges and buy yourself some lunch,* the note read.

He'd have to go out for the milk and the fruit, so it looked like he was free to roam. What could go wrong in the daylight anyway?

He decided to walk the length of the Boulevard, scouting out the town on foot, then pick up the groceries on the way back.

First he'd get an early lunch.

A man was working on his car in the alley behind the building, bent over the open hood. Dad had obviously driven to Jersey City instead of taking the bus, since their parking spot was empty.

The weather had cleared and it was a lot warmer, but there were puddles all over the sidewalk as he walked up the Boulevard, which was filled with people walking.

He passed the YMCA and several small groceries and restaurants and clothing stores. At Eighth Street he reached Jalapeños.

He could see through the door that the restaurant was already busy, mostly men sitting alone or in pairs at small, square tables. At the front of the store was a counter with several dishes on a steam table. The food smelled spicy and delicious.

Jimmy stepped inside. A young woman behind the counter smiled at him.

"Ramiro here?" he asked.

"Ramiro, *sí*," she said. She pointed toward a half-door with a sign that said EMPLEADOS SOLAMENTE. Jimmy could see that it was the kitchen, with a steel table and sink and a large stove.

Ramiro came through the door and grinned. "Thought I heard my name," he said. He was wearing a white apron.

Jimmy pointed toward the sign on the door. "Does that mean kitchen?"

"No," Ramiro said. "That means 'You ain't allowed.' Employees only."

"Oh."

"What are you up to?"

"Was hungry. What's good here?"

"Everything's good. What do you like?"

"Most things." Jimmy nodded toward a table, where two men had plates of yellow rice and beans and chicken. "That looks great."

"*Arroz con pollo,*" Ramiro said. "It's good and it's cheap. We sell it by the ton."

"I'll have that then."

"You'll like it. I'll be back in a few minutes."

Jimmy took a seat at one of the tables near the front. All of the tables had white tablecloths with yellow flowers printed on them, and all of the cloths were covered with sheets of clear plastic. The woman at the counter brought him a plate of the food and some utensils.

"Drink?" she asked.

Jimmy looked at the cooler of bottles beside the counter. The words Coke and Sprite were the only English words he saw in the whole restaurant. So he ordered a Coke and started eating.

The food was tasty and there was a lot of it.

Jimmy tried to read the menu while he ate, but he didn't know much Spanish.

Ramiro came out and sat across from him. "Good?" he asked.

"Great."

"I work until two. You want to come back then and hang out in town?"

"Yeah. Definitely."

"We'll find something to do. Maybe play some basketball."

"Good deal."

Jimmy chose the Bonanza Supermercado to get the groceries: CARNES, FRUTAS Y VEGETALES. Big posters filled all of the front windows: EXTRA LARGE EGGS/HUEVOS, RICE/ARROZ 20-POUND BAG, GREEN PLANTAIN, FRESH BEEF TRIPE. He didn't know what plantains were, and he didn't think he *wanted* to know what tripe was.

He walked down a very narrow aisle stacked to the ceiling with cans of beans and tomatoes and bottles of olive oil; dog food; baby food; and cereal. There were dozens of types of beans, mostly in cans labeled GOYA or LA FE. Mops and brooms for sale hung from the ceiling.

In the back of the store was a meat counter, and alongside that some produce bins. He put four large oranges in a paper sack, found the dairy case for a half-gallon of milk, and took a can of red beans just for the heck of it. Then he paid at the front counter and headed for home.

Ramiro was out in front of the restaurant when Jimmy returned, dribbling a basketball and wearing a yellow baseball cap backward.

"How much you work?" Jimmy asked.

"Just weekend mornings. Most of us work at least some—my brothers and cousins."

"You get to cook?"

"Not for customers. I know my way around the kitchen, though. I make my own stuff sometimes when I'm hungry."

"I wouldn't mind being a cook," Jimmy said. "I like being around food."

They walked to the YMCA, which had an outdoor basketball court around back. Several high-school kids were playing a half-court game at one basket. Jimmy swallowed hard when he saw

Spencer and Lamont and a few other seventh-graders down at the other end, just shooting. They were all quite sweaty; they must have been playing for a while.

"Phlegm alert!" said Spencer when he spotted Jimmy.

Ramiro smacked hands with Spencer, who was giving Jimmy a smirk. "What's been good?" Spencer asked.

"With me?" Jimmy asked.

"Yeah, you."

"I don't know." He wasn't even sure what Spencer meant.

"You don't know what's good?"

The other kids were standing close, looking Jimmy over. They'd seen him many times, of course, but always in school or at practice. This was the first time he'd come close to hanging out.

"It's finally getting warm," Jimmy said. "That's pretty good."

"Yeah," Spencer said. "The weather's gonna do what it do. . . . You got some height. You play hoops?"

"Of course."

"Maybe you can handle Jared—he's our center. Me and him'll take Ramiro. You be with Lamont and Willie."

Jimmy shrugged. "Whatever you say."

Spencer and Jared had been starters on the school basketball team and played together well. Jared had a couple of inches on Jimmy and a bit of bulk, so he had no trouble scoring off feeds from Spencer.

"We smashed you," Spencer said after hitting a long jumper to win it. The game hadn't been close. Jimmy managed just two baskets against Jared, who had scored almost at will.

"Quicker game than out in Ohio, huh?" Spencer asked.

"Pennsylvania," Jimmy corrected. "Home of Temple, Villanova, LaSalle. The Sixers? You ever heard of them?"

Spencer laughed. "Philly's a long way from the Poconos, though. Ain't it?"

Jimmy shrugged again. "I guess. . . . Sturbridge is more of a football town."

Jared shook Jimmy's hand and said, "Nice

game." His T-shirt said HUDSON CITY SUMMER LEAGUE. Jared was the only other white kid in the game, but he fit right in. He and Spencer seemed to be just about best friends.

Spencer walked over to the chain-link fence at the side of the court and uncapped a bottle of Gatorade. He sat on the asphalt and took a drink. Then he ran his fingers through his hair, which wasn't very long, and stretched out his legs. "I'm done," he said. His skin was dark against his plain white tank top, and his muscles shone with sweat. "Toss me that top," he called to Willie, who picked up Spencer's sweatshirt and threw it at the fence.

Lamont and Jimmy teamed up for a two-on-two game against Ramiro and Jared, which they lost but were much closer.

"I gotta leave," Jimmy said, figuring that his father would be home soon.

"Me, too," said Jared.

"I'm out," said Lamont.

So Jimmy walked off while the others gathered their stuff. No one had quite said good-bye, although they'd kind of acknowledged that he was leaving. City kids were different, but not *so* different, he figured.

He looked back as he reached the gate. Ramiro had his back to him, talking to Spencer and laughing. Lamont caught Jimmy's eye and pointed at him, holding his finger out and nodding quickly. They were all waiting for each other; they'd leave together and get sodas or go to someone's house to hang out.

But Jimmy felt all right. The game hadn't ended up in a fight or an embarrassment. He hadn't made much of an impression either way, but nobody had given him grief. Just Spencer's usual routine.

He wasn't a great basketball player, but anything athletic was Jimmy's best way of relating to other kids.

He'd be okay. It wouldn't be easy, but he'd find a way to fit in.

# 5
# Opening Day

*T*he first day of April was bright and warm, and Jimmy could hardly contain his excitement as he and Ramiro tossed a ball back and forth. In just a few minutes the season would begin. They were nervous and excited, even though they'd be starting the game on the bench.

Jimmy felt a rush of pride as he looked at Ramiro's bright-red cap with HC emblazoned on the front. He was wearing that same cap and the same white uniform with the red pinstripes and socks.

Neighboring Union City was visiting on this

Wednesday afternoon, and the bleachers held a reasonable number of spectators. The base paths on the dirt diamond were lined in white, and the not-quite-green grass had been neatly trimmed. The digital scoreboard beyond the center-field fence was lit up with zeroes.

"Let's go!" called the umpire, and the Hudson City starters trotted onto the field. Jimmy and Ramiro entered the dugout, where they stood behind the protective chain-link fence, their fingers gripping the links.

David Choi had taken the mound for the Hornets and was throwing his final warm-up pitches to Jared. Spencer and Lamont and the other infielders whipped a ball around the horn. The Union City leadoff batter stood in the on-deck circle, intently watching David's delivery.

The umpire shouted, "Play ball!" and the batter stepped up to the plate.

"No batter!" Jimmy yelled, picking up on the infield chant. "He can't hit!"

But he could, and he lined David's first pitch into the gap between left field and center. The speedster rounded first and slid into second way ahead of the throw, popping up quickly and dusting off his pants.

"Settle down!" Coach Wimmer called. "No problem. No problem."

A groundout moved the runner to third, and a single to center brought in the first run of the season. David walked the next batter, but then settled down and managed to get out of the inning with only the one run scoring.

Jared doubled home Lamont to tie the score in the bottom of the first, but after that the Hornets came up dry. Union City managed hits in every inning and gradually built a lead. It was 4–1 when the Hornets came up to bat in the bottom of the fifth of the seven-inning game.

"You two," Coach Wimmer said, pointing toward Ramiro and Jimmy, "start warming up. David's thrown a lot of pitches. We're going to need you."

So they took a ball and left the dugout, moving behind the metal bleachers outside the field. There was no bullpen here; they just found an uncrowded spot and threw the ball back and forth, warming up their arms.

After a few minutes they heard a solid crack of the bat and a roar rising up from the spectators. Jimmy turned and ran around the bleachers just in time to see the ball soaring over the fence. Spencer was running from first base toward second, his fist raised in the air. He'd hit a two-run homer. Hudson City was just one run behind.

Jimmy followed Ramiro quickly to the dugout. Their teammates were cheering Spencer and smacking his back.

"That's what I'm talking about!" Lamont said. "That shot was too good."

Coach told Ramiro he'd be pitching the sixth inning. "We're still in this game," he said. "Keep us close."

"Come on, man," Jimmy said, punching Ramiro lightly on the arm. "We've got momentum now."

And Ramiro started well, striking out the first batter he faced and getting the second to pop out.

But then he seemed to lose his concentration, walking two batters in a row and falling three balls behind on the next one.

Coach Wimmer called time and walked to the mound. Ramiro kept nodding as Coach talked. He kicked at the dirt and bit down on his lip.

The next pitch was way outside, and Jared had to lunge to keep it from getting past him. So the bases were loaded.

Coach looked over at Jimmy. "You ready, Flem?" he asked.

"Yeah."

"Good. This next batter is his last. You're going in."

Jimmy gulped and nodded. He wanted to pitch, but he felt bad for Ramiro.

Jared was out on the mound, talking to the pitcher. He patted Ramiro on the shoulder, then turned and trotted back to his position.

Ramiro threw a strike, and that apparently made him relax. He nodded his head slowly, let out his breath, and gave the batter a determined look.

The batter swung fiercely at the next pitch but

failed to make contact. Ramiro then struck him out with a fastball and walked swiftly toward the dugout.

"Nice job!" Coach said as Ramiro hurled his mitt onto the bench.

Ramiro sat down hard and pulled his cap down low over his forehead. "That was terrible," he said softly.

"You pulled it together," Coach said. "No harm done, right?"

"Right."

"You kept us in the game. Good work."

Jimmy sat next to Ramiro and said, "Way to bounce back."

"Yeah, I guess. After I walked the whole team."

"Three guys," Jimmy said. "And they didn't even score."

Lamont came over from the corner of the dugout and spoke to Jimmy. "Somebody wants to see you," he said, gesturing to the left.

Jimmy stepped over to the fence and saw his dad standing there in a jacket and tie.

"Just got here," Dad said. "You play any?"

"I'm about to. I'm pitching the seventh."

"Great. You can get the win if your guys can score a few runs."

Jimmy gave a tight smile and exhaled hard. He was feeling enough pressure already.

"Saddle up and go," Dad said.

"Saddle up and go," Jimmy repeated.

He jogged to the mound, pounding his left fist into his glove. The Hornets still trailed, 4–3. It was up to him to shut down Union City and keep the team within striking distance for the bottom of the last inning.

Jimmy looked around the infield. His eyes locked with Spencer, who gave him a playful look and made that hacking sound again, spitting and smiling. "Grind time," Spencer said. "Time to get us a W."

Union City had the top of its batting order coming up. That leadoff hitter who'd doubled on the first pitch of the game stepped in, taking a few practice cuts and glaring out at the mound. He'd also hit a single and had scored two runs.

Jared signaled for a curveball, and Jimmy

nodded in agreement. He went into his slow windup, bringing the ball way back, then zipping it forward with that overhand motion and whipping it toward the plate. It caught the outside corner and the umpire yelled, "Strike one!"

A supportive cheer went up from Jimmy's teammates. "No batter!" they called. "Heavy phlegm!"

Jimmy rubbed his forehead with two fingers, holding the ball in his glove. The batter was crouched lower now, his mouth slightly open and his eyes fixed hard on the pitcher.

Jimmy threw a low fastball and the batter swung, connecting with the ball but sending it harmlessly out of bounds.

"Straighten it out, Blue," came a cry from the Union City dugout.

The advantage was clearly Jimmy's now. At 0–2, the batter couldn't afford to let any close pitch go by. Jimmy would keep it low and inside. *Don't give him anything good to hit.*

But as soon as the pitch left his hand, he knew it would be trouble. The ball was moving fast, but it was waist-high and right down the middle. The batter swung cleanly and knocked it past Lamont for a single.

Jimmy took the throw and studied the base runner. The guy was fast; he'd be looking to steal. *Concentrate on the batter,* Jimmy thought, but that was easier said than done. The runner took a good lead and looked like he was ready to spring. And Jimmy's next pitch was low and wild, skipping past Jared and bouncing off the backstop. The runner easily made it to second.

Jared called time and trotted out to the mound. "Settle down," he said, handing Jimmy the ball. "Forget the base runner. Let's get this guy out."

Jimmy threw a hard fastball, and the batter squared to bunt. The ball was nudged forward and Jimmy ran in to field it. He looked toward third base, but the runner was already sliding in. So he turned and threw to first for the out.

And just like that, Union City had set up another run. Unless Jimmy could get a strikeout or an infield pop-up, they were almost certain to score.

He looked toward his dad, who shook his fist and shouted, "Gut check!"

*All right,* Jimmy thought. *Let's see what I'm made of.*

He had started to sweat, a good sign, and was angry that he hadn't kept the ball down to that first batter. Now the guy was dancing on the third-base line, smirking at Jimmy, certain that he'd score again. "Blue," they called him. Odd name.

Third-baseman Miguel Rivera darted to the base and Jimmy faked a throw in that direction, sending Blue right back to the bag. Jimmy would make sure he stayed there. He fired a fastball toward the plate, and the batter swung and missed. The second pitch was a ball, but the third flew right past and smacked into Jared's glove for strike two.

Same situation. Jimmy was ahead of the batter. *Nothing good to hit,* he thought. *No creampuff pitches like that other one.*

The pitch was smooth, low, and a little outside, but too close for the batter to chance it. He swung and missed. Strike three! Two outs.

"Yeah!" yelled Ramiro from the dugout, where he was standing along the fence. The infielders increased their chatter now. They were one out from their last at-bats.

Jimmy pumped his fist toward his chest and took the throw from Jared. He squinted at the runner on third with a defiant glare. Blue gave the same look back. He took a half-step toward home plate, crouched low and ready to run.

Union City's cleanup hitter stepped in. He was a strong kid and had twice sent Willie back to the fence in center for long fly-outs. He clearly had the power to hit one out of the park.

Strike one.

Ball one.

Ball two.

Strike two.

Jimmy squeezed the ball and wiped his face with his mitt. Everyone in the park was standing now. His mouth was dry.

This was the pitch. This would do it. As he brought the ball forward he felt it slip slightly from his fingers, just enough to make his stomach sink.

It was low, it was outside, and it was spinning away from Jared.

The ball bounced in the dirt and skidded toward the backstop. And here came that runner, full speed toward the plate. Jimmy rushed in and grabbed for the ball as Jared tossed it, but Blue was sliding low and Jimmy couldn't make the tag in time. He'd scored.

The batter grounded out on the next pitch and the inning was over, but the damage had been done. Three bad pitches. That was all it had taken to give Union City a run.

The Hornets scored once in the bottom of the seventh, but that made it even worse for Jimmy. If he'd pitched a clean inning then the game would be tied. But he hadn't been able to do it. The Hornets had lost, 5–4.

"I blew it," he said to Ramiro. "Two wild pitches and a big, fat creampuff."

Coach was upbeat despite the narrow loss, but most of the players were mad. They'd come so close. Nobody said anything negative to Jimmy, but he could feel what they were thinking. He knew he'd let them down.

He left the field with his dad, who put his hand on Jimmy's shoulder and squeezed. "You threw some good pitches," he said.

"Yeah. And some mighty bad ones."

"As long as you learn from it," Dad said. "You can't just groove one down the middle to a hitter like Blue."

"I didn't *groove* one, Dad. You make it sound like I did it on purpose."

"You should have kept it low and inside. Don't let him get so much wood on the ball."

"I *know*, Dad. Sometimes knowing what to do and actually doing it are two different things."

They walked in silence the rest of the way, and they stayed quiet while Dad cooked some chicken and carrots. Jimmy put on the TV and watched the end of a *Simpsons* rerun.

Dad gave him a smile when they sat down to eat. "There'll be plenty more games," he said. "By the way, I found *two* pens uncapped when I stopped here after work this afternoon. The one by the phone and another one out on the kitchen table."

"So what?"

Dad shrugged and lifted a forkful of carrots to his mouth. "No big deal. But they dry *out,* Jimmy. And the caps get lost if they're not attached to the pens."

Jimmy stuck his fork into the chicken. "Who cares?"

"Yeah. Who cares? But pens do cost money."

"You gotta be kidding me, Dad." Jimmy shook his head and looked at the ceiling. He knew this couldn't really be about the pens. "You're mad because I blew the game."

Dad laughed. "I am *not* mad."

"Admit it. You hate it when I don't perform like a hero."

"That's not true," Dad said evenly. "I would never put that kind of pressure on you."

Jimmy looked down at his plate. "Sure, you wouldn't."

"I wouldn't."

"Right, Dad."

"Let's forget it."

"Right." Jimmy salted his chicken and took a swig of milk.

Dad cleared his throat. "I just thought you knew better than to throw that kind of pitch to a hitter like Blue."

"See! This *is* about the game."

"No . . . It's not. I'm sorry. Really. I just want those kids to like you, Jimmy. I want you to fit in."

"You think they'll like me if I *pitch* better?"

"No. I know it's not as simple as that. You know what I mean; kids are tough on newcomers."

"No kidding," Jimmy said sarcastically. He stood and walked toward his room.

"You didn't eat much," Dad called.

"Too bad."

He stayed in his room for an hour, steaming. He knew his dad was quirky, but this thing with the pens was going overboard. And Jimmy knew that getting kids to like him would take more than pitching well. That kind of thinking was way too shallow.

He was hungry now, so he went out to the

kitchen and made a peanut-butter sandwich. Dad was in the living room reading the newspaper, but he didn't say a thing.

Jimmy took his plate and walked over to the couch, sitting down in a huff. He picked up the remote and turned on the television, glancing out of the corner of his eye at his father. Certain that his dad was watching, he very deliberately set the volume at 19.

There was more than one way to get things done. The right way, the wrong way, and a million different ways in between.

# 6
# The Real Deal

Friday afternoon the Hornets dropped their second game in a row, losing at Hoboken, 3–2. Jimmy and Ramiro never left the dugout. Miguel Rivera pitched the entire game and kept it close, so Coach Wimmer didn't even have the relievers warm up.

"Nothing worse than sitting out a whole game," Jimmy said as they made their way to the bus.

Ramiro just shrugged. "Yeah, but at least we're on the team."

"True." But Jimmy had been hoping to make an impact today, to have good news to bring to his mother. He'd seen her only once in the past six weeks. Tonight he'd be leaving to spend the weekend with her.

Dad was waiting in the car when the team's bus pulled into the middle-school parking lot, and they drove up through Weehawken and onto Route 3, making their way past motels and fast-food places and warehouses and Giants Stadium. They were nearly to Route 80 before Jimmy realized how hungry he was.

"Can we get some hamburgers or something?"

"Sure," Dad said. "I just wanted to get a good head start. I'm driving all the way back tonight."

"I know."

They grabbed some food at a Wendy's drive-through and ate their dinner on the way. Dad had been mostly quiet since they left Hudson City. He crumpled up a hamburger wrapper and asked, "Did your coach even realize that you didn't play?"

"I don't know. What difference does it make?"

"Well, I think everybody should play, no matter what the score is. Don't you?"

Jimmy didn't answer. That sounded like a little-kids rule to him. When he played YMCA soccer or Little League ball, there were rules to make sure everyone played. But this was different. This was the real deal.

Dad cleared his throat and switched to the fast lane to get around a truck. "You should've spoke up."

"What do you mean?"

"Tell him you needed to play. Tell him you were ready to pitch or play the outfield or pinch-hit or *something*."

This was bad advice and Jimmy knew it. The last thing a coach needed to hear in the midst of a tight game was that some scrub wanted to play. That was sure to keep him right there on the bench for the rest of the game and probably the next one.

"Come on, Dad. You played sports. You know that sort of thing just makes you look like a baby."

Dad kept his eyes on the road for a few seconds, then turned and peered over his glasses at his son. "Maybe I should talk to him."

"No *way*, Dad! It was one game. He'll use me when he needs me."

"If he remembers that you're sitting there."

"Dad, just keep out of it. Miguel pitched a good game. Why should Coach have pulled him?"

"All I know is I would have got you in there. . . . Heck, if I was calling the shots you'd be starting."

Jimmy held his tongue and looked out the window. The terrain was starting to look more familiar, more like Pennsylvania. Lots of wooded hills and even some small farms. They were getting close to the Delaware River.

All he needed was for his Dad to interfere. Coach would be all right about it, but he'd never hear the end of it from guys like Spencer and Miguel. That'd be a ticket to disgrace.

"Just stay out of it," Jimmy said. "Please don't turn into one of those dads."

They didn't say much the rest of the way to Sturbridge, winding their way up dark, forested Route 402 past Marshall's Creek and Bushkill and Lake Wallenpaupack. Dad didn't even get out of the car when he left Jimmy off, he just pulled into the driveway, beeped the horn, and said, "See you Sunday night. Have a good time. I love you."

Mom met Jimmy at the door and hugged him tight. He could smell cookies baking—that was a rarity—and classical music was playing softly. She asked him about school and baseball and said he looked great. She told him he needed a haircut; maybe he could get one tomorrow at Mick's. He could walk downtown, get lunch at the diner, stop in to see Marty at the sporting-goods store—all those things he missed doing in a town he'd known all his life.

He said he was tired, but they stayed up late and watched a movie—she'd rented three of them at Blockbuster because she wasn't sure what he'd already seen.

Later she made herself a cup of tea and brought him some orange juice.

"Dad's been driving me nuts," he finally said.

"How?"

Jimmy stared at the TV—an ancient rerun of *The Honeymooners*—and sighed. "He thinks I'm a baseball star. Or at least that I *should* be. I'm just glad to be on the team."

"He knows you love baseball."

"Yeah, but it's not my whole life. He's constantly giving me advice or thinking I should be in the starting lineup. It's like it's *his* whole life."

Mom rolled her eyes and took a sip of tea. "He always did go a little overboard about you and sports. . . . Some unfinished business from his own 'career.'"

"Yeah. He never quite made it, huh?"

"Not quite."

On TV, Norton was teaching Ralph to do "The Hucklebuck" dance so he could make up with Alice. Jimmy laughed.

Mom asked if he'd made any friends in Hudson City. He thought for a moment and said, "Sort of." It made him wonder how she was doing. She'd always had friends, but how did she feel about living by herself?

"You get lonely?" he asked.

She gave a tight smile and looked at him fondly. "I miss you. A lot. But you know I keep busy.

I was always *too* busy for you, wasn't I?"

"It was okay. I was busy, too."

It was strange a while later to walk up the stairs to his bedroom. This had been home for so long— forever, as far as he was concerned—but now it felt like revisiting a memory. The walls of his room were filled with items from his not-so-distant past: a mounted trout that he'd caught in the Lackawaxen River, an honor-roll certificate from last year, a class photo from fourth grade, a plaque from a Little League championship.

This wasn't quite home anymore, and Hudson City wasn't quite yet. Would it ever be?

He sat on the bed. Dad had been the coach of that Little League team, the one that finished third in the regular season but raced through the playoffs and came out on top. Jimmy was the star pitcher, the cleanup hitter, the captain. Only two years ago.

Dad the coach. The cook at home. The guy who was always there. Mom worked all day, rode her horse in the late afternoon, went to meetings of the arts council or the Democrats or the library board at night. She was a good person. She just wasn't there much.

Home was with Dad, wherever that turned out to be.

But home was also back here. How could he have it both ways?

# 7
# Feeling the Heat

*T*op of the seventh. Game tied. David had walked two batters in a row and Coach decided that he'd had enough.

"Let's go," he said to Jimmy, signaling to the umpire for time and leading the way onto the field.

Jared, Miguel, Spencer—they were all gathered around the mound, looking concerned. Hudson City had built a 3–0 lead early, but David yielded a game-tying homer the inning before and seemed to have lost his rhythm. He handed the ball to Jimmy with a quick nod and walked toward the dugout.

There was one out. Jimmy threw a half-dozen warm-up pitches and waved to the umpire that he was ready.

"Shut 'em down!" Spencer said. "We'll win this thing in our next ups."

The fielders went back to their positions and Memorial's big catcher stepped up to the plate. Jimmy looked over toward Dad, leaning forward in a middle row of the bleachers.

His first pitch was a strike, moving quickly and nicking the outside corner. *Just like that,* he thought. So he threw the same pitch, a little lower but well within the zone. The batter watched it go by for strike two.

"That's the boy!" yelled Miguel. "Flem brought his 'A' game today."

*Yeah*, Jimmy thought. *I'm on.*

Now he'd bring the real heat. The big delivery. The pitch felt great as it left his hand, ripping toward the plate. But the batter swung smoothly and connected, lining the ball toward right-center. It skipped once and bounced off the fence, sending Willie and Ryan scrambling.

The runner from second made it all the way home, and the one from first slid safely into third.

Still only one out, the lead gone, and two men in scoring position. Jimmy exhaled hard and looked up at the sky.

He avoided looking at his father as he waited for the ball.

"No problem," said Spencer, but the enthusiasm was missing.

The next batter hit a long fly ball to center. Willie got under it and easily made the catch, but the runner from third tagged up and scored.

Two batters faced, two runs in. Jimmy felt sick. His hands were trembling.

And now he couldn't find the plate. His next three pitches were high and away. Jared called time and trotted to the mound.

"What's going on?" Jared asked.

"Nothing."

"Gotta get your head together, Flem."

"I stink today."

"Just throw a strike. This guy won't swing at a 3–0 pitch."

Jimmy blinked hard and nodded. "Probably."

He got the next one over the plate, but then walked the batter with a fastball that nearly nicked him in the shin.

A first-pitch single loaded the bases. Coach Wimmer came out to the mound.

"Hit a little rough spot, huh?" he asked.

"I guess."

"Had enough?"

Jimmy kicked gently at the mound with his toe and looked down. "I messed up," he said under his breath.

Coach pointed toward Ramiro in the dugout and waved him onto the field. "Gotta stop the fire," he said to Jimmy. "Just one of those days."

Jimmy bit his lip as he walked off. He got to the dugout and huddled in the corner, pulling his cap down and staring at his mitt. He couldn't believe how bad he'd pitched. Four batters: a double, a run-scoring fly-out, a walk, and a single. Couldn't have been much worse.

Ramiro pitched a clutch strikeout to end the inning, but the damage was done. Three Hornet batters went down in order in the bottom of the seventh and Memorial had a big comeback win. Hudson City was 0–3.

"We just ain't that good, are we?" Miguel said as they all sat in the dugout, waiting for the coach to return.

"I'm not hearing that noise," Spencer said. "We've been close in every game. *So* close. Don't go telling me we're awful."

Coach sat on the step facing the players on the bench. He rubbed his chin and smiled. "We must be the best 0–3 team in the state," he said. "A couple of runs here or there and we'd be 3–0. But that's baseball."

Dad was waiting when he left the dugout. Jimmy was angry, mostly at himself, but he knew he'd probably start crying if he spoke. His contributions to the team so far had been miserable.

"What happened out there?" Dad asked.

Jimmy looked away. "I don't know," he said softly.

"That was some opportunity," Dad said.

"Yeah. And I blew it, right?"

"Well . . ."

Jimmy started walking. "You think I need you to tell me that?" he said sharply as Dad caught up. "You think I don't know?"

"Hold on," Dad said. "I wasn't criticizing you."

"Oh, no?"

"I was going to try to help."

They reached the street and turned toward the Boulevard. Jimmy didn't respond.

Dad cleared his throat. "Maybe we can figure out what happened."

"I *know* what happened, Dad. They pounded me."

"I mean *why* it happened."

"Why I choked, you mean?"

"Well, I wouldn't put it that way."

"Put it any way you want. That's what went down."

"Listen," Dad said, but Jimmy cut him off.

"Drop it, all right? I don't *want* to talk about it and I don't *need* to talk about it. I just need to think for a while. Okay?"

"Whatever you say."

Jimmy stopped walking. "I'm going back," he said.

"To the field?"

"Yeah. I just want to be alone. Get it?"

Dad frowned, but he didn't fight back. "Fine. Be home by dark and I'll have supper ready."

Jimmy walked back toward the field and entered the chain-link fence. A few players were still milling around and Coach Wimmer was looking at the scorebook. Jimmy leaned against the fence and stared out at the diamond.

He'd never fit in here. So much traffic, so much noise. Kids his age who seemed two years older. No room to unwind, to walk out of town and see deer and rabbits and smell cows in the fields. Too much pressure from his father.

He'd thrown some good pitches after taking the mound. But that first hit had really rattled him. He'd been afraid to give up another run. But that had happened anyway.

"You all right, Flem?" Coach asked as he spotted him.

"I guess."

"Don't sweat it. You just lost your nerve for a few minutes. . . . I'm sure it's around here somewhere."

Jimmy gave a halfhearted laugh. "It better be."

"We'll get you back on the horse. There's another game in two days."

"Thanks."

He went back to the Boulevard and turned left, walking quickly past their building and heading downtown. The after-work traffic was heavy and pedestrians were going in and out of stores and cafés. He was thirsty but not ready to go home.

After six blocks or so he heard his name, and turned to see Ramiro and Willie coming out of a grocery store with bottles of juice. Like Jimmy, they were still in their uniforms and carrying their mitts.

"What are you doing down this end of town, Flem?" Ramiro asked.

"Just walking."

"Are you lost?" Willie said with a smirk.

Willie and Ramiro were two of the shortest guys on the team, but both were good athletes.

Jimmy responded to Willie's remark. "Wish I was," he said.

"What's up?" Ramiro asked. "Your dad tell you not to come home or something?"

"No. I just didn't want to go there. I don't feel like hearing him tell me how I messed up."

"So you're a fugitive?" Willie said, still having fun.

Jimmy laughed. "Nah. Just taking a breather."

"Come on," Ramiro said. "I was gonna show Willie my new fish. You want to see?"

"Why not?"

Ramiro lived in a narrow two-story brick house just off the Boulevard. They climbed the front steps and Ramiro opened the door with his key. They stepped into the living room and Jimmy recognized the aroma of rice and beans and chicken cooking, so similar to what he'd eaten at Jalapeños. On a wall was a small shelf with figurines of saints. Another wall held dozens of framed photographs of people and tropical scenes.

A small older woman looked out from the kitchen and said, *"Hola."*

Ramiro turned to Jimmy. "That's 'hello' to you," he said. "This is my *abuela*. Grandma, *es* Jimmy *y* Willie."

She smiled sweetly and hugged Ramiro. They spoke in Spanish to each other for a moment, and then Ramiro led the boys upstairs to his room.

"New swordtails," he said, pointing to one of three fish tanks.

Jimmy glanced at the tanks, but he was more interested in the walls filled with posters of singers and athletes. He studied a framed map of Cuba. "You from here?" he asked.

"Sort of," Ramiro replied. "I've never been, but my parents were born there. My grandparents, too."

"They all live here now?"

"Yeah. Every inch downstairs has something about Cuba in it. Music, pictures, you name it."

"They wish they could go back?"

Ramiro shrugged. "I don't know. They love it here. It's like they have two homes—this one here, and the one they might never go back to. You know what I mean?"

"I think so."

"I mean, I've lived my whole life in Hudson City, but even I feel some roots back there. In Cuba."

Willie tapped on one of the tanks. "That one's pretty," he said, pointing to a red-and-blue fish.

"That's a neon."

"These things hard to take care of?" Willie asked. "I might want to get some."

"Not hard. I like it. You just want to give them a good environment. Clean and calm, not too much light. You know. Make them feel at home."

They studied the tanks for a few minutes. Ramiro shook some food from a small container into one. "You got to watch which types of fish you put together," he said. "Some of them don't get along."

"You train 'em?" Willie asked.

"Nah." Ramiro laughed. "They ain't like dogs or people. If a fish don't like another fish, you can't make 'em change."

Jimmy and Willie left a few minutes later, walking in opposite directions on the Boulevard. It was nearly dark now, and all the streetlights were on. Many of the stores and restaurants had their doors propped open, and Latin music was pumping out to the street.

He was hungry. *Arroz con pollo* would be good, but his dinner would be strictly American. Dad had said he'd be making pork chops and broccoli.

Maybe they'd watch a baseball game tonight. Or probably two of them. It wouldn't hurt to study the pitchers. He might even learn something.

# 8

# The Wrong Guy

*T*hings didn't improve for the baseball team that week as they dropped their fourth straight game. Again, Jimmy was on the mound in the crucial moments. And again, he didn't come through.

He hurried out to practice on Thursday, not because he couldn't wait to get there, but because he didn't want to hang around the hallways and be confronted by any teammates. No one had said much after the game—they were all too stunned— but he'd heard a few rumblings in school today that maybe Coach needed to find a different left-handed relief pitcher.

So he was one of the first players to reach the field. David and Ryan were throwing a ball back and forth on the infield. Spencer was sitting alone in the dugout, reading the weekly *Hudson City Observer*. Middle-school sports never got much press, but there was a brief article about the baseball team's latest loss.

"You see this?" Spencer asked Jimmy, rattling the paper.

Jimmy sat next to Spencer and pulled the paper toward him. He looked at the headline and winced.

### ROUGH START FOR MIDDLE SCHOOL NINE

By Phil Glick
Staff Reporter

The Hudson City seventh-grade baseball team surely knows the meaning of heartache. Every game the team has played this season has been agonizingly close, but the results have always been the same.

The team is 0–4 after its latest loss,

4–3, to Palisades yesterday afternoon.

"We're playing pretty well," said longtime Hudson City coach Don Wimmer. "We're just not getting the breaks."

The Hornets held a 3–2 lead entering the final inning of yesterday's game, but Palisades managed a two-out rally in the bottom of the seventh to steal the victory. Reliever Jimmy Fleming took the loss. Fleming pitched well in the sixth, but yielded a walk and a double in the seventh. Both runners later scored on a throwing error, and the game was history.

"That's how it's been all season," Wimmer said. "We get so close we can taste it, but something manages to take it away."

Starting pitcher Miguel Rivera had a triple for the Hornets, and Spencer Lewis added a two-run homer. The Hornets play on the road again on Monday against league-leading Union City.

Spencer took the paper from Jimmy and folded it up. "Looks like you get all the blame," he said.

Jimmy stared out at the field. He felt bad enough about the game without everyone in town reading it in the paper. He'd barely slept that night. He didn't need Spencer rubbing it in.

"They mentioned my homer," Spencer said.

Jimmy kept staring. Willie and Lamont and some others had arrived and were jogging in the outfield.

Spencer rolled up the paper and smacked it against the cinder-block wall of the dugout. "One thing I don't like is when the wrong guy gets credit for something," he said. "And I like it even worse when the wrong guy gets the blame."

Jimmy turned to Spencer, who was looking at him hard. Spencer had made that error, turning what should have been a game-ending throw to first into a disaster.

Jimmy had begun the inning with a strikeout, then walked a batter on a close 3–2 pitch after a series of foul balls. He'd then yielded a double, but came back with a three-pitch strikeout to bring the team one out away from victory. That's when Spencer made the wild throw, whipping it way past Eddie at first base where it bounded off the fence and into right field. By the time Ryan chased it down and threw it home, two runs had crossed the plate.

"Don't think for a second that I don't know where the blame goes," Spencer said. "I blew it. I blew it big-time. You pitched great."

"Thanks," Jimmy said softly. He nodded. "I did all right."

"You did more than all right, Flem. Everybody here knows it, too."

Jimmy put up his fist and Spencer met it with his own. "Don't beat yourself up over that error," Jimmy said. "If you hadn't hit that homer we would have lost anyway."

"I ain't down," Spencer said. "All I mean is, the paper gave you a bad rap. They should have said who made the error. I can take it."

"I can, too," Jimmy said. "They can write what they want if it's the truth."

Coach had arrived and called everyone onto

the field. He had them run a few laps, then they worked on fielding ground balls and pop-ups. Everyone seemed listless and uninspired.

Coach had seen it all before. He tried to keep things moving, but the players were just going through the motions. He joked a little, as usual, and didn't dwell on the most recent loss or the record. But he stopped practice half an hour early and told the players to go home and forget about baseball for a few hours.

"You all look like your dog died," he said. "Forget the game. Go eat cookies or pizza or something. Watch cartoons on TV. You even have my permission to smile."

Coach knew that his team was a good one, that the players had talent and heart and good attitudes.

There was just one thing they were lacking.

They were badly in need of a win.

# 9
# A Secret Ingredient

Another weekend, another two-hour drive to Pennsylvania. Jimmy and his mom went out to the movies this time. Sunday morning they went to church for the first time in months. That afternoon they had dinner at the Sturbridge Inn.

Surprisingly, he found himself missing Hudson City: his room overlooking the back alley, the hustle and noise of the Boulevard, even the kids from the team. Spencer's words had meant a lot. He felt like less of an outsider. So what if the team was losing? At least he was a part of it.

So he was glad when Dad pulled into the driveway in their old red Escort, beeping the horn twice. Jimmy kissed his mom and told her he'd had a good time.

Dad was talkative on the way home, telling Jimmy about work—things were going well, but he'd have to go to the office a few evenings this week—and mentioning a new recipe for pork stew he wanted to try making.

"What's the secret ingredient?" Jimmy asked. There was always a secret ingredient, something Dad added to recipes as his signature contribution.

"I'm thinking it might be maple syrup."

"In a stew? Sounds very weird."

"Yeah, but I think it might work. I'll try just a little. If it's good, we'll add more next time."

They hadn't talked about baseball for several days. Dad had been to the Palisades game but hadn't said a word about it. They both knew it was too painful to talk about.

So Jimmy was the one who brought it up, waiting until they'd crossed into New Jersey and both of them had been quiet for a while.

"I feel like my fastball's moving pretty well, despite . . . everything," he said.

Dad's eyes got a little wider, and he nodded a few times. "I noticed. You've been striking out a lot of batters."

"Yeah. That's true."

"Your coach seems to have faith in you. I mean . . . he keeps using you."

"Even though we're losing. Yeah. He seems to be okay about it."

Jimmy looked out the window. Things were starting to turn green—new leaves on the trees. The hills here in the Delaware Water Gap region were steep and forested. The traffic on Route 80 was light.

"How are the kids holding up? Your teammates getting discouraged?"

Jimmy could tell what Dad really meant: Was anyone getting on him about giving up the lead in two straight games?

"They're okay," Jimmy said. "Everybody knows we've been right there in every game. Just coming up short."

"So no one's too upset?"

"Well, we all hate losing. But I know what you're asking, Dad, and the answer is they've been fine to me. Spencer especially—the guy who busted my chops in the beginning. He's honest, at least. He acts like he's the king sometimes, but he knows when he's messed up and he owns up to it."

"That's good. There are a lot of professional athletes who won't do that."

They were quiet for a while after that, just listening to Dad's Bob Dylan CD and watching the scenery. They were nearly to Montclair before Dad spoke.

"You know, I never really was much of an athlete," he said. "I *wanted* to be. Oh boy, did I want to be. I guess that's why I push you a bit, since I figured you wanted it as much as I did and had a better chance of succeeding."

"Yeah, but what made you think I'd be better than you were? Wouldn't you think I'd just inherit your . . . um . . . talents?"

Dad laughed. "Or my *lack* of talent. Sure, heredity is a big part of it. But you've got two sets of genes in you. At least one of your parents was a good athlete."

"Mom?"

"She never talks about it, but she was quick and strong. Basketball, softball. Even tennis. So I figured you must have some of that in you. And if I pushed you to work at it, you'd succeed."

"Makes sense, I guess."

Dad tapped the steering wheel with his knuckles. "I think the biggest factor is the athlete's heart. How hard he'll work with what he's given."

"I work pretty hard."

"I know that. It makes me really proud."

"Makes me proud, too, I suppose," Jimmy said. He hadn't thought about it much, but just giving his all meant something. He wasn't a bad pitcher. And he *was* getting better.

He opened his gym bag and took out the mounted trout he'd brought back from his mom's house. "Remember this guy?" he asked.

Dad laughed. "The monster of the Lacka-waxen! That was the day my waders sprung a leak and I nearly got frostbite in my toes."

"Yeah." Jimmy dug into the bag and took out the Little League photo. "Brought this, too," he said.

"Champions," Dad said. "Some run, huh? *That* was a team with heart."

"I know it."

"What made you bring all that stuff?"

Jimmy shrugged. "My roots," he said. "Need to add a touch of my home back there to my new home here in New Jersey."

Dad swallowed and blinked. "That makes sense," he said softly. "Everything works out, you see?"

Jimmy just said, "Yeah," and put the trout back in the bag.

Sooner or later it all works out. Jimmy thought about that a bit. As far as he was concerned, it was true.

# 10
# Forever and Three Days

*J*immy stood in the narrow area of dirt between the fence and the step down to the dugout, gritting his teeth and watching intently as Coach Wimmer walked out to the mound. Would he let Ramiro finish this inning?

Hudson City trailed, as usual, 3–0, and Union City was threatening to widen the gap. Ramiro had just yielded a double, and Union City runners were poised safely at second and third. There was only one out in the bottom of the fifth, and the top of the order was coming up. That meant Blue, who had riddled the Hornets with three hits in the season opener and two more today.

Jimmy was ready—he'd warmed up for several minutes while Ramiro struggled through the past two innings. And now Coach was waving him onto the field, sending Ramiro to the dugout.

Jimmy took a deep breath and jogged past his friend, who was shaking his head and frowning as he left the mound. The other infielders were gathered around Coach Wimmer, waiting for the new pitcher.

"Got to stop the flood," Lamont said to Jimmy.

"Gotta get this guy," Spencer said. "Grind time. Too many *L*s on our record already. Time to get that *W*."

Jimmy took the ball from the coach and squeezed it hard. Spencer poked his glove into Jimmy's side. "Been forever and three days since this team won a game," he said. "We gotta smash."

Jimmy nodded. The team was foundering, but all he could do was pitch. He glanced at the runner on second, then the one on third, then glared in at the batter.

His first pitch was high and outside, and Jared had to stand to catch it. There were a few groans from the Hudson City spectators, but mostly an excited murmur from the Union City fans.

Blue smirked as he looked at the mound. He had a double and a single today. He was also pitching, and had allowed only a handful of base runners.

Jared signaled for a fastball, and Jimmy felt a surge of energy. He leaned back and wailed one past Blue, who watched it go by for a strike.

"That's the one!" called Lamont.

"Our turn now," said Spencer. "No batter."

Blue inched closer to the plate and waggled the bat, squinting as he focused on the pitcher. Jimmy threw another fastball. Blue smacked it toward second base.

Spencer darted toward the grounder and extended his glove, snaring it behind second and whipping it to first. The throw beat Blue by half a step for out number two, but the runner from third had scored.

Jimmy looked at the sky and shook his head.

Now it was 4–0, and another runner was on third. He'd never been on a team that lost five straight games.

"All right, all right!" called Spencer. "We got the out. Now let's get one more."

Jimmy took the throw from first baseman Eddie Ventura and sized up the next batter. It was the Union City second baseman, who'd bunted successfully against Jimmy in the first game. He wouldn't be bunting now, with two outs and a man on third. He'd be hitting away.

Or trying to. Jimmy threw two quick strikes and the batter didn't come close. Now the curve, nicking the outside corner and popping into Jared's glove. Inning over.

Jimmy walked toward the dugout, excited but mad. He'd pitched well, but Hudson City had a mountain to climb. Four runs down to the best team in the league.

"That's what I'm talking about!" Spencer exclaimed as he caught up to Jimmy and wrapped an arm around his shoulder. "We shut them down. Now let's get us some runs."

But Blue struck out the first two batters he faced before Willie Shaw finally drew a walk.

Willie had speed. With Spencer coming up to bat, Coach gave Willie the sign to run. So he was halfway to second when Spencer lined the first pitch deep into right-center. The ball bounced off the wall and squirted away from the fielder, who tracked it down and hurled it toward the infield. Willie crossed the plate and shook his fist as Spencer slid into second.

They'd finally broken through for a run.

Blue toed the mound and looked disgusted. But he nodded when the first baseman called, "They got lucky. No more!"

Lamont drew a walk, but Eddie Ventura struck out on three pitches to end the inning. Blue gave a smile toward the Hudson City dugout and strode with confidence off the mound.

Jimmy hustled onto the field. His pitches had been moving, and he was ready for more. Plus, he'd be batting second in the top of the seventh, right after Jared. Could they get three runs and tie this game up?

He shook off Jared's signal for a curve; he wanted to bring some heat. Three straight fastballs did the job: nicking the outside corner for strike one, keeping it high and inside but drawing an awkward swing for strike two, and then a blazing pitch right down the middle for the out.

There was lots of noise from the infielders, lots of excitement. Spencer's run-scoring double and Jimmy's sudden dominance on the mound were infectious. The second batter grounded out to second, and Jimmy finished the inning with another three-pitch strikeout. The Hornets ran to the dugout determined to win the game.

"Right over the fence, Jared," said Willie as the Hudson City catcher stepped up to the plate.

Jimmy put on a batting helmet and wiped his hands on his pants. He took a couple of practice swings, then kneeled in the on-deck circle.

Blue's first two pitches were balls. He seemed to be putting a lot of effort into every pitch. Jared smacked the third one over the second baseman's head, and it landed safely in right field for a single.

Jimmy took a deep breath and walked to the

plate. Relief pitchers didn't get to bat very often; this was his first time up all season.

He tried to catch the pitcher's eye, but Blue was all business. His first throw was to first, trying to pick Jared off. But Jared easily slid in.

"Heavy phlegm alert!" shouted Spencer from the dugout, but this time it didn't sound mean at all. It sounded supportive.

Jimmy watched a low fastball go by for ball one. He stepped back and looked quickly toward the third-base coach, wondering if he should try to bunt Jared over to second. But there was no sign. Down by three runs in the final inning, Hudson City needed base runners.

Blue's next pitch was fast but outside, and the chatter from the Hornets' dugout increased. "Good look, Flem!" "A walk's as good as a hit."

He took the third pitch for strike one. Blue gave a sharp nod and pounded his glove.

*No more waiting,* Jimmy thought. *If it's a good pitch you have to swing.*

Blue seemed to exaggerate his windup now, bringing forth an extra effort and sending a wicked fastball toward the plate. Jimmy swung hard and made contact, drilling the ball on a line drive that landed foul beyond first base.

A low curve brought the count to 3-and-2. Jared would be running. Jimmy gripped the bat tighter and dug in. All of the Hornets in the dugout were standing, urging him to clobber this pitch.

The ball was coming hard but it didn't look good. He had to decide in a fraction of a second: Swing or wait? Strike out or walk?

He didn't lift the bat. The ball landed in the catcher's glove with a solid *smack.* But the umpire called, "Ball four!"

Jimmy turned, rolled the bat toward the dugout, and trotted to first base as his teammates cheered. Blue sneered and shut his eyes. His coach called time and walked to the mound.

Miguel was up now. He had some power and could tie the game with one swing.

The Union City coach walked back to the dugout. Blue was staying in.

"He's tired, Miguel!" called Willie. "Wait for your pitch."

Willie was right. Blue was clearly laboring as he

threw two fastballs that were both high and out-side. Miguel called time, stepped out of the batter's box, and adjusted his helmet. He checked his bat-ting glove and spit off to the side. Then he stepped back in and lined Blue's pitch on the ground toward first base.

The first baseman fielded the ball and had a decision to make: throw to second and try to nail Jimmy or run to first for the out. Jimmy was sprinting as hard as he could and was ready to dive toward the bag. So the fielder made the easier play and got Miguel out.

Jimmy was sprawled face-first on top of sec-ond, his hands in the dirt and his feet in the air. He looked toward third, where Jared was safely in scoring position. One out, men on second and third, and David coming up to bat.

Blue turned and gave Jimmy that look that said, *You ain't going nowhere*. But sometimes you just sense a shift in a ball game, or maybe even a shift in the way an entire season is pointing. Jimmy felt that now. They could win this game. They could win a lot of them.

David muscled the next pitch right up the

middle for a single and Jared easily scored. Jimmy rounded third but the coach yelled to hold up. The center fielder had been playing shallow and had already thrown to the infield.

So now it was 4–2 and Hudson City had the tying runs on base. Ryan Grimes was coming up for the Hornets, and Blue was finished pitching. The Union City coach was bringing in a big left-hander.

Instead of going to the dugout, Blue walked to third base as the coach went over the lineup changes with the umpire. The third baseman went out to left and the left fielder went to the dugout. Blue stood next to third base with his hands on his hips, a foot away from Jimmy, while the new pitcher took a few warm-up throws.

Jimmy turned toward Blue, who gave a hard stare back but then smiled. "You guys don't want this game to end, do you?" he asked.

"Not if we can help it," Jimmy replied.

"Better hope you get lucky." He motioned toward the mound. "This boy throws *hard.*"

Ryan, the right fielder, was the weakest hitter in the Hornets lineup. He swung wildly at two quick pitches, then let a third one go by for a called strike.

"See what I mean?" Blue said with a smirk.

Jimmy shrugged. "That's just two outs," he said. "It'll be three."

"Looks who's up."

Blue rolled his eyes as he saw Willie standing at the plate. "That short guy."

Willie had a small strike zone and a good eye; Blue had walked him twice today. And when the first two pitches were high for a 2–0 count, Blue shouted, "Concentrate!" to the pitcher.

Jimmy looked over to David at first base and made a fist. David made one back. They were ready to run.

The next pitch brought an "Oooooh," from the crowd as the umpire called ball three. It had just missed.

Willie tapped the plate with the bat, set up, and watched a strike go by. Now he crowded the plate a little tighter and crouched a bit, making the target even smaller. The pitcher was rattled. The ball was way high and outside.

Jimmy clapped his hands as Willie ran to first.

The bases were loaded for Spencer.

"This guy," Blue said with mock disgust, knowing full well that Spencer's double had given the Hornets life the inning before. He took a step in, nearly to the infield grass, and said, "Right by him, Lefty."

Spencer took a strike and shook his head slowly, as if to say, *Try that again, pitcher. You'll be sorry.*

The next pitch was a ball, and Jimmy felt as if the whole scene was compressing. As if the whole frustrating season was riding on this next pitch: make or break. Fall to 0–5 or start over fresh.

Spencer stepped toward the pitch, made a clean, powerful swing, and connected with the most solid and satisfying wallop Jimmy had ever heard. He crossed the plate in seconds, turned and watched as David sprinted down the line and scored, and shouted as Willie rounded third, everyone hollering as the ball soared in from center field, the catcher blocking the plate as he waited for the throw.

Willie and the ball arrived at the exact same

moment. Willie slid into the catcher, who had grabbed the ball and was knocked off his feet, landing on top of the runner and tagging him with the ball.

The umpire yelled, "Safe!" and Willie leaped to his feet. David and Jimmy embraced him, jumping up and down. The Hornets players rushed from the dugout to greet them. They'd taken the lead. It was 5–4.

Spencer stood on third base, beaming and dancing. Blue stood rigidly next to him, staring toward home plate.

The Hornet dugout was wild, players smacking each other on the back and hugging. Lamont was at bat. Ramiro grabbed Jimmy's arm. "You ain't done yet," he said.

"Oh, yeah," Jimmy said with a smile. Union City still had to bat.

And there was no time to catch a breath. Lamont hit a weak pop-up to the second baseman to end the inning. Ramiro gave Jimmy a gentle shove. "Get out there," he said. "Shut 'em down."

The first batter popped out, but Jimmy walked

the next one. A groundout moved that guy to second. There were two outs, but a single would probably tie the game.

He glanced toward the third-base line, just beyond the Hudson City dugout, and caught his dad's eye. Dad nodded slowly. Jimmy bit down on his lip and scratched his chin. *Saddle up and go.*

The batter was left-handed, tall and thin. He had a nervous stance, fidgeting and blinking as he waited for the pitch. Jimmy threw hard and nearly hit him.

"No batter!" the infielders called, and this time it seemed to mean something. *Forget about this guy; just get the ball over the plate.*

Jimmy threw a strike, hard and low. He let out his breath as Jared tossed the ball back. *No problem,* he thought. *No problem. Just throw another one like that.*

And he did, but the batter was smart. He saw that pitch coming and jumped on it, lining it up the middle for a hit.

Jimmy's stomach tightened as he turned and watched the ball dart out of the infield. The runner from second was at top speed, heading for third with no thought of stopping. Willie fielded the ball in center and threw it hard toward the plate.

Jared was poised to make the catch as the runner raced down the third-base line. The ball bounced between the mound and the plate, but it was right on target. The runner slid, Jared pounced, and everyone in the park waited for a split second that seemed like forever for the umpire to make the call.

"You're out!"

That was all the Hudson City players needed to hear. Those in the dugout came running onto the field, yelling and smacking hands with the fielders. Jared trotted out and wrapped his arm around Jimmy's neck as Lamont and Spencer whacked him on the arm and the shoulder. They'd broken through. They'd finally won a game.

Now they felt as if they'd never lose again.

# II
# A Winning Tradition

*E*ven though it was a Monday evening, Spencer insisted that as many players as possible go out to celebrate the victory.

"Just an hour at some grub spot," he said. "Who's up for it?"

Jimmy and Ramiro and several others said they'd go, and a few more said they'd come by after dropping in at home for a few minutes. So ten players crammed into two tables pushed together at the Villa Roma pizza place on the Boulevard—a favorite hangout for Hudson City athletes—and munched on pizza and wings.

"We got nine more games until the playoffs," Spencer said, raising a glass of soda. "We better win 'em all or there won't *be* any playoffs for us."

"We got the monkey off our backs now," David said, his mouth full of pizza. "That seventh inning—that was the real us."

"You said it."

Jimmy sat back and looked around at the group. White, Black, Hispanic, Asian; short and tall, skinny and muscular. Their faces were dirty, their hair messed up. But they all were wearing the same uniform. They were definitely a team.

He'd been tested. A lot. He hadn't passed every test, but how much did that matter? Here he was, among teammates and friends. A long way from home. Or was he?

"How're the fish?" he asked Ramiro, who was playing with his drinking straw, holding one finger over the end so the soda would stay inside when he held it aloft.

Ramiro let the soda squirt back into his glass. "They're good," he said.

"Not fighting?"

"Nah. They glare at each other from tank to tank, but they're all safe where they are. I don't mix them up. You do that, you find 'em floating the next day."

"I hear you."

Jimmy picked up a chicken wing and sucked some of the sauce from it. "So who's paying for all this?" he asked.

"Tradition," Spencer said with a grin. "The tradition is that the winning pitcher picks up the check. I think that's how it goes."

"Hmmm," Jimmy said, smiling back. He could tease, too. "I think I heard it differently. I always thought it was the guy who got the game-winning hit that paid the bill. Especially if it's a three-run triple."

Spencer beamed and shook his head. "I ain't hearing that noise, Flem. Maybe we can split it. . . . Ten ways."

"Sounds like a plan." Jimmy reached for another wing. He grabbed a couple of napkins, too. Didn't want any sauce on his uniform.

He leaned back and had two slices of pizza

while his teammates ribbed each other back and forth about their haircuts and their accents and girls that some of them liked. Cow country or city, it didn't really matter. When a team played hard and triumphed, the feeling was the same.

There was nothing better than a victory celebration.

He had a feeling there'd be many more to come.

* * *

# Read an excerpt from

# Dunk Under Pressure

## Winning Season #7

Dunk leaned forward on the bench, his hands clenched and his eyes intently watching the action on the court. Fiorelli was dribbling quickly across midcourt, head up, looking for an open man. Hudson City was ahead by four with just over a minute to play.

Fiorelli passed to Spencer in the corner, and Spencer dumped it in to Jared under the basket. Jared gave a quick head fake and the Camden center bought it, leaving Jared an opening for an easy layup.

Dunk stood with the others and yelled. The game had tightened up in the second half, but a six-point lead in the final minute was big.

Camden called time-out and the Hudson City players ran to the bench and gathered around Coach Temple.

"Defense," he said. "This one's not over yet. Ryan, take a seat." Coach looked around. "Dunk, report in."

"Me?" Dunk asked, his eyes wide.

"Do it."

Dunk reported to the scorer's table and trotted back to the coach, who put his hand on Dunk's shoulder. "If they score, Fiorelli will in-bound the ball to you. Camden needs to foul or we'll just run out the clock. Protect the ball. Let them put you on the line."

Dunk swallowed hard and stepped onto the court. He looked at the clock: 57 seconds.

With a six-point lead, Hudson City expected the opponents to try for a quick three-pointer. So they were surprised when Camden's point guard passed the ball inside to the center, who banged home a layup.

"No problem," Spencer shouted as Fiorelli took the ball under the basket.

Dunk darted toward the end line. The Camden

players were pressing, desperate to get the ball back, but Dunk was free and he took the pass and turned to dribble.

Two Camden players converged on him, stabbing at the ball and blocking his path. The ball was knocked loose, but an official blew his whistle, calling a foul.

Camden was over the foul limit. Dunk would be shooting two.

"Money in the bank," Spencer said, punching Dunk lightly on the shoulder.

"Automatic," said Fiorelli, jogging next to him toward the basket.

Dunk bit down on his lip and stepped to the line. His heart was pounding and his breathing was rapid, even though he'd only been in the game for a few seconds. His sweat felt cold.

He bounced the ball once, shut his eyes and opened them. Checked his feet and eyed the rim.

The shot fell short, barely grazing the rim and falling to the floor. Worst shot he'd taken in months. The crowd groaned.

"No problem," said Spencer. "Forget them jitters, Dunk."

The second shot was true, softly falling through the net and raising the lead to five points. The Hudson City players ran back on defense. Camden charged up the court.

The spectators were all standing now, pumping fists and screaming.

Willie and Spencer hounded the guards as they moved the ball around the perimeter, needing to shoot but cautious not to force one.

Dunk was near the basket, guarding a forward. The man darted out toward the free-throw line, then cut quickly back and headed toward the corner. Dunk tried to follow but ran squarely into the Camden center, who was setting a screen to free his teammate.

The pass went to the corner, and that forward was open. The three-pointer rolled around the rim and fell in. The lead was down to two.

Twenty seconds remained. Fiorelli faked a pass to Spencer, and Dunk's man took one step too many in that direction. So Dunk was open for the in-bounds pass, and Fiorelli got him the ball. Again came the quick foul.

Dunk wiped his hands on his jersey and blinked. He felt like he'd swallowed some rocks.

Make two shots and this game was over. Miss one and Camden would still have a chance.

Dunk looked at the Hudson City bench, where his teammates were smiling, confident of the victory.

"All you!" shouted Coach Temple.

"Ninety-nine percent!" said Lamont.

Dunk's hands were shaking as he took the ball from the official. His armpits were dripping. This wasn't his driveway. It wasn't an empty court at the Y.

He knew the first shot was off the instant it left his hands, drifting left and bonking off the side of the rim.

Dunk took a deep breath to steady his nerves. Twenty thousand shots last year. Now all he needed was one.

The second shot looked good to him, arcing over the rim, right in the middle. It looked good to everybody in the gym.

But it wasn't. An inch too far, it hit solidly off

the back of the rim and floated just beyond the front. Players leaped for the rebound, and Jared got there first, tapping it hard.

In the scramble that followed, the Camden point guard came up with the ball, skipping past Spencer and Fiorelli and finding an open court ahead. The spectators were counting down the seconds—six, five, four—as Dunk and the others gave chase.

The guard had time for a layup and the path was clear, but he decided to take a chance. He stopped his dribble, faced the basket, and unleashed a perfect three-pointer that dropped cleanly through the net for the lead.

That was it. The horn sounded before Fiorelli could in-bound the ball. A six-point lead in the final minute had vanished completely. The Hudson City players stood there stunned as the Camden players went wild.

Dunk felt like he could melt right there. They'd been counting on him—the free-throw special-ist—and all he did was choke.

★ ★ ★

**RICH WALLACE** was a high school and college athlete and then a sportswriter before he began writing novels. He is the author of many critically acclaimed sports-themed novels, including *Wrestling Sturbridge, Shots on Goal,* and *Restless: A Ghost's Story.* Wallace lives with his family in Honesdale, Pennsylvania.